For John and Andi

ISBN 978-0-545-39065-1

Copyright © 2010 by Doug Cushman. All rights reserved. Published by Scholastic Inc., 557 Broadway, New York, NY 10012, by arrangement with Henry Holt and Company, LLC. SCHOLASTIC and associated logos are trademarks and/or registered trademarks of Scholastic Inc.

11 12 13 14 15 16/0

40

12 11 10 9 8 7 6 5 4 3 2 1

Printed in the U.S.A.

First Scholastic printing, October 2011

Designed by Elizabeth Tardiff

Watercolor and ink on Lana watercolor paper were used to create the illustrations for this book.

Halloween Good Night

Doug Cushman

SCHOLASTIC INC.
New York Toronto London Auckland
Sydney Mexico City New Delhi Hong Kong

When day turns to night with stars overhead,
All Mommas and Papas tuck their kids into bed.
But if you were a monster on Halloween night,
How would you wish your momma and papa **good night?**

If you were a **werewolf** on the moor's muck and mire,
Near an old gypsy cart and a smoldering fire,
With a full yellow moon shining its ghastly moonlight,
How would you tell your hairy papa **good night?**

If you were a **creature** in the dark Black Lagoon,
Snug in your swamp 'neath a watery moon,
Gurgling bubbles as you snuggle in tight,
How would you tell your scaly mommy **good night?**

If you were a **mummy** in a sarcophagus bed,
Wrapped up in linen from your toes to your head,
What would you say in the orange torchlight,
How would you wish your mummy mommy **good night?**

If you were a **skeleton** in a graveyard of stones,
Clacking and rattling all your dry, bleached-out bones,
Yawning a yawn in the ivory moonlight,
How would you tell your bony daddy **good night?**

If you were a ghost haunting a castle and moat,
Rattling thick chains, making underpants float,
When you stopped all your moaning and screeching in fright,
How would you tell your phantom papa **good night?**

Boo! Boo!

Boo! Boo!

If you were a **witch** with a bubbling brew
Of frog hairs and worm feet and the tongue from a shoe,
When this foul-smelling potion is seasoned just right,
How do you tell your black kitty **good night?**

If you were a **vampire** in your box in the tomb,
As your papa—the Bat—flaps his wings 'round the room
Before he flies off to find someone to bite,
How would you tell your sharp-fanged papa **good night?**

Screeech!

If you were an **alien** in a spaceship from Mars,
Exploring some galaxies, planets, and stars,
Snug in your sleep tube traveling faster than light,
How would you tell your Martian mommy **good night?**

Across the whole world monsters short, thin, and round,
In castles, lagoons, and deep underground . . .

Tuck their kids into bed and pull the blankets up tight.
So how do **you** tell your momma and papa **good night?**

GLOSSARY

ALIEN: ⳡ⳾:⼁⌂⌇⳪◻⧸⤲

BENGALI: শুভরাত্রি
(shubhoratri)

CREATURE: Glug! Glug!

DUTCH: Goede Nacht
(khowdeh nahckt)

FRENCH: Bonne nuit
(bun newee)

GERMAN: Gute Nacht
(gooteh nahckt)

GHOST: Boo! Boo!

GREEK: Καλή νύχτα
(kalinihta)

HEBREW: לילה טוב
(laylah tov)

ITALIAN: Buona notte
(bwona nottay)

JAPANESE: お休みなさい
(o-ya-su-mee-na-sa-ee)

MANDARIN: 晚安 *(wahn ahn)*

MUMMY: 𓊹𓂝𓏏𓊮𓈖𓈖

PORTUGUESE: Boa noite
(bohah noytch)

RUSSIAN: Доброй ночи
(dobroy nochi)

SKELETON: Clickity-
clackity-clack clack!

SPANISH: Buenas noches
(bwenas nohches)

URDU: شب بخیر
(shub bakhair)

VAMPIRE: Screeeech!

WEREWOLF: Yowwll!

WITCH: Hee! Hee!

DOUG CUSHMAN

has illustrated more than a hundred books, including *The Amazing Trail of Seymour Snail*; the *New York Times* best seller *What Dads Can't Do*; his own Dirk Bones books and the Aunt Eater mystery series, as well as *Mystery at the Club Sandwich*, for which he received a California Young Readers medal. In researching this book, Doug wrote to the British Museum for the correct hieroglyphs for "good night" and even used some tombstones he discovered on a trip to Transylvania as models for the graveyard scenes. He lives in Paris. [www.doug-cushman.com]